THE
MAN-BEAST

The Man-Beast

ISBN-13: 978-1944540470

For information about production rights, visit:
www.jzettelmaier.com

Published by Sordelet Ink
Cover by David Blixt

THE MAN-BEAST

A PLAY BY
JOSEPH ZETTELMAIER

SORDELET
ink

THE MAN-BEAST premiered at First Folio Theatre, in Oak Brook, Illinois on April 8, 2016. It was directed by Hayley Rice. Set design by Angela Weber Miller. Lighting design by Michael McNamara. Costume design by Rachel Lambert. Sound Design by Christopher Kriz. Prop Design by Vivian Knause. Violence designed by Rachel Flesher, assisted by Zach Payne. Stage managed by Julia Zayas-Melendez, assisted by Gillian Garrett. Produced by David Rice.

The cast was as follows:

VIRGINIE - Elizabeth Laidlaw
JEAN - Aaron Christianson

For information about production rights, visit www.jzettelmaier.com.

CAST OF CHARACTERS
JEAN CHASTEL, 50S, A HUNTER
VIRGINIE ALLARD, 40S, A TAXIDERMIST

TIME
JUNE, 1767

PLACE
VIRGINIE'S CABIN
GÉVAUDAN PROVINCE, FRANCE

ACT I

SCENE ONE

(Lights rise. The interior of a small taxidermy shop. It is a wooden shack, filled with a large variety of trophy animals, posed to look fearsome. It is lit by candles and lanterns. A large carving table is centerstage, blood-stained, with a variety of taxidermy equipment around it. Suddenly, a loud banging is heard at hear door)

JEAN
(Outside) Help! HELP!

(He hears no response and tries to open the door. He slams into it with his shoulder, forcing himself inside. He is a tall, strong man in his 50s, dressed in leathers. He holds one arm, which is bleeding. He is clearly in pain)

JEAN
Please...I need help...anyone? ANYONE?

(He looks around; clearly no one is home)

JEAN
…merde…

(He heads to the counters, knocking over items in search of something. He finds a bottle)

JEAN
…have to do…

(He pulls the cork out with his teeth, then downs a mouthful of the liquor)

JEAN
Un, deux, tois…

(He pours the liquor on his wound and howls in pain. He hits the table with his good hand)

JEAN
GOAT-FUCKING WHORESON!

(He finds a needle and tries to thread it, but it is very difficult with his wounded arm. VIRGINIE walks in, carrying a basket of plants. She is dressed in peasant clothes. She sees JEAN & grabs a musket near the door)

VIRGINIE
AY! What's this then!?

(He turns, and she points the musket at him)

VIRGINIE
Who are you!?

JEAN
Please help me…

VIRGINIE
Who!?

JEAN
I've been bitten! I need your...

VIRGINIE
Step into the light.

JEAN
I don't...?

(VIRGINIE points to a lit candle on the table. JEAN walks to it so she can see his face)

VIRGINIE
Craggy bastard, aren't you?

JEAN
Help me, woman.

VIRGINIE
I know you, yes?

JEAN
Help me, woman!

VIRGINIE
Chastel. Jacques Chastel.

JEAN
Jean Chastel.

VIRGINIE
You're the hermit. The other hermit. You live ten miles past the creek.

JEAN
Will you help me or no!?

VIRGINIE
Listen to you bark! You, who forced yourself into my home, and... *(She notices the bottle)*...and drank my damned wine!

JEAN
I had to wash out the wound!

VIRGINIE
(Speaking to the stuffed bear) Isn't this a thing? I was
collecting some foxglove, and I come home to find this
great lummox bleeding on my floor!

(JEAN starts to stagger towards her. She pulls a knife)

VIRGINIE
Back!

JEAN
...please...

VIRGINIE
I gutted a fat boar just yesterday, and I imagine you'd
be easier.

JEAN
I know who you are.

VIRGINIE
Ha!

JEAN
You're the woods witch. The heathen.

VIRGINIE
Is that what I am?

JEAN
They say you can heal.

VIRGINIE
Better than that fat barber in Gévaudan. He doesn't
know a proper stitch from...

(He reaches into his pockets, tosses some coins on the ground. Pause)

VIRGINIE
Got more?

JEAN
Plenty's there.

VIRGINIE
The way you're bleeding, you'll need many a stitch. Stitches aren't free.

(He lumbers towards her. She backs up, knife drawn)

VIRGINIE
Slow now.

JEAN
Woman, if I die on your floor, know that I will rise up and haunt you til your last day.

(Beat. The woman laughs, and stabs her knife into the table)

VIRGINIE
I bet you would at that.

(She grabs JEAN and with some effort manages to push him onto her table. They talk as she removes his coat and shirt)

VIRGINIE
Christ, you're no little one.

JEAN
Careful...

VIRGINIE
Got to wash you up first. See if it's as bad as it looks.

JEAN
Just do it!

VIRGINIE
Bit?

JEAN
Eh?

VIRGINIE
You said you were bit?

JEAN
Oui. A wolf.

VIRGINIE
You fool hunters. Wolves a-plenty here. Best to… *(Beat. She backs up)* You were hunting The Beast, oui?

(He doesn't answer)

VIRGINIE
A bunch of damn fools, the lot of you!

JEAN
Stitches…

VIRGINIE
And you saw what? A Loup-Garou? A wolf that walks as a man…or a man as a wolf?

JEAN
Stitches now.

VIRGINIE
I don't know what bit you, but if you think…!

JEAN
STITCHES NOW!

VIRGINIE
Oui. The stitches.

(She pushes him down on the table. She takes some water and cleans the wound. He cries out)

VIRGINIE
Quiet, you mewling babe. It's just water.

JEAN
It stings, you whore!

VIRGINIE
Whore? But I don't charge for it. (She examines the wound) You were wolf-bit?

JEAN
Oui.

VIRGINIE
And this was the bite?

JEAN
Non, I bit myself and blamed the wolves. STITCH IT UP!

VIRGINIE
It's barely broke the skin! The way you were carrying on, I thought I'd have to take your arm off!

JEAN
Christ! Were you going to...?!

VIRGINIE
Sometimes an arm comes off. But not this time. Here. (She shoves a leather belt in his mouth) Bite hard or you'll spit out some tongue before I'm done. Ready? (He nods) Breathe deep.

(She begins to sew. He screams through the belt, moves

a little bit. She grabs his face)

VIRGINIE
Keep still, damn you. Or you'll bleed all over my finery.

(He nods. She goes back to work. He struggles to stay still. She whistles as she works, clearly used to this)

VIRGINIE
I know, I know. Not as nice as a hand on your cock, but you'll survive.

(She gives the string a hard tug. He cries out)

VIRGINIE
Poor thing. *(She wipes blood off his arm and her hands)* I ate tar-tar once. Didn't bleed as much as you.

(He pounds on the table)

VIRGINIE
You've a nice look about you. If you die, I may have to stuff you and put you with them. *(She motions at the trophies)* Almost done. Almost. *(She quickly ties up the stitches)* There. *(She slaps the wound. He grunts)* Tough like old leather, you are.

(He spits out the belt)

JEAN
You're more butcher than healer.

VIRGINIE
Truly. *(She wraps up his arm with a bandage)* Little nip like that, you might not even get a scar. But if it goes rotten, put maggots on it. Should rid you of the bad flesh.

JEAN
Wine. Give me wine!

VIRGINIE
Give me coin and I'll give you wine.

(He hurls more coins on the ground. She hands him a bottle. He begins to drain its contents)

VIRGINIE
I meant to spend the night stuffing a red fox for Etienne LeMarque. You know him? Baker in town. Pays me in pastry as often as gold. Well, he brought me a fox his boy'd shot and...

JEAN
For god's sake, woman! Do you ever shut your flapping jaws?!

(Beat. She thinks about it)

VIRGINIE
No. Mayhap when I sleep. But I'm asleep then, so I can't speak for certain.

(He tosses her the empty bottle)

VIRGINIE
The whole damned bottle?

JEAN
I'll take more if you have it.

VIRGINIE
My wine is for me, M'sieu Chastel. *(Beat)* So tell me.

JEAN
Tell you what?

VIRGINIE
What really bit you, hmm?

JEAN
The Beast. The very Beast itself, or god strike me down.

VIRGINIE
Pffft. If it was a Loup-Garou that bit you, then it would've done worse than that. Know you what I think?

JEAN
...I'm about to...

VIRGINIE
I think big, brave Jean Chastel ran afoul of a neighbor's dog...

JEAN
Ha!

VIRGINIE
...and spun a story to save his pride. "The Beast!" Jean cried. "La Loup-Garou, big as the devil and twice as ugly!" When in truth, was no more than some mangy cur.

(He examines his wound and stitches)

JEAN
Is it true you're a witch?

VIRGINIE
Does that matter?

JEAN
It may.

VIRGINIE
Hear tell you're no godly man yourself. It's why they run you out of town, same as me.

JEAN
I don't care what you worship. But do you know... things?

VIRGINIE
(Smiling, she shrugs) I know a thing about a thing.

You're worried about the bite.

JEAN
(*Nodding*) I've heard tales.

VIRGINIE
La loup garou. When one gives you a nip, you become one yourself. Now tell me.

JEAN
Tell you what?

VIRGINIE
Tell me what you saw!

(*Beat. JEAN starts to put his shirt back on*)

JEAN
Big.

VIRGINIE
How big?

JEAN
Ten stone at least. Maybe even fifteen.

VIRGINIE
Big as that?

JEAN
Came at me on all fours At first I thought it was a bear, but...the sound it made. Like a scream, and a howl, and... (*Beat. He reads her expression*) You've heard it before.

VIRGINIE
We live in the woods. The woods are full of sounds. Who's to say...?

JEAN
You have. A roar from Hell itself.

VIRGINIE
...mayhap. It...it matters not. Were you hunting it?

(He says nothing)

VIRGINIE
The King's offering good gold to the man who kills the thing. No shame in it.

JEAN
I was hunting it.

VIRGINIE
Then you must be the greatest hunter in all of France. Not a single man has seen it, much less gotten bit.

JEAN
I had it in my sights. I put a musketball straight into its heart. It dropped...and it got back up as though nothing had happened.

VIRGINIE
You didn't use silver. Has to be silver to kill a loup garou.

JEAN
Truly?

VIRGINIE
So they say. You should've come to me first. I know a thing about a thing.

JEAN
You should've been hunting it yourself.

VIRGINIE
Ha! If such a thing is real, then I prefer my blood and bowels inside my body. Gold is worth less to the dead.

JEAN
I had the Beast! I had it!

VIRGINIE
That torn arm tells me a different story.

JEAN
Weeks! I spent weeks tracking it, finding its hunting ground! All for naught!

VIRGINIE
Every hunter in fifty miles can say the same.

JEAN
But none found it! I found it! I, Jean Chastel! Those whoresons in Gévaudan spit on me, call me godless, but not a one of them could do what I did.

VIRGINIE
They all failed. You just failed AND got bit.

(He turns on her)

JEAN
Three years that creature has been killing us. Villagers eaten and rent apart. I cannot even say how many...

VIRGINIE
One hundred and thirteen.

(Beat)

JEAN
Truly?

VIRGINIE
Etienne told me himself, just today. Last one was poor Marie Decaud. They found her a week ago, her head ripped clear off her neck.

JEAN
Too many gone.

VIRGINIE
The way I hear it, you have no love for the people of
Gévaudan. What do you care how many the beast feeds
upon?

JEAN
My reasons are my own.

VIRGINIE
Your reasons make a pretty jingling noise in a coin
purse.

JEAN
You do not know me, woman.

VIRGINIE
Nor you, me.

(Beat. She offers her hand)

VIRGINIE
Mem'selle Virginie Allard.

(He stares at her hand, doing nothing)

VIRGINIE
You'll not shake the hand of the woman who saved
your life?

JEAN
You didn't save my life.

VIRGINIE
Is that so?

JEAN
It is so.

VIRGINIE
Let me undo those stitches, then. See how fast you
bleed out.

(Beat. He shakes her hand)

JEAN
Avec plesir, Mem'selle Allard.

VIRGINIE
You don't come to manners easily, but you do come
to them.

JEAN
When it suits.

VIRGINIE
Here. Come. *(She takes him towards her shelves. She
talks as she searches for something)* You best be careful.

JEAN
Why?

VIRGINIE
You shot the beast and it lived. Might well be hunting
you now.

JEAN
Good. The sooner I see it, the sooner I collect my gold.

VIRGINIE
Oh! The gold is yours already, is it?

JEAN
Only a matter of time.

VIRGINIE
Confidence is one thing, m'sieu, but...Ah! *(She finds
some moss on her shelves. She hands it to him)*

Toothed peat moss. Put that on the wound. Leave it there a day and a night.

JEAN
Why?

VIRGINIE
In case I'm wrong about the bite. If the Loup Garou passed its disease onto you, the moss might soak it out of the wound.

JEAN
You said I'd be well!

VIRGINIE
I said I knew a thing about a thing. True wisdom is born from mistakes.

JEAN
Christ... *(He unwraps his arm, puts the moss on it, and rewraps the wound)* You best play me fair, woman.

VIRGINIE
Did I charge you for the moss? That's more than fair, I say.

JEAN
Hmmph.

VIRGINIE
We're not so different, thee and me.

JEAN
Fine.

VIRGINIE
It's god's truth! Both of us live in the wilds because there's no other place for us. The men of Gévaudan hate you as they hate me, and for the same reasons!

JEAN
Not the same!

VIRGINIE
Pah!

JEAN
I may be a godless man, and proud of it, but you...
you're a...

VIRGINIE
A witch?

(Beat)

JEAN
It's true, then. You're a bride of Satan.

VIRGINIE
Ha! You see a ring on this finger? I'm no man's bride,
no devil's neither.

JEAN
This place stinks of witchcraft.

VIRGINIE
Mayhap it does. I know a thing about a thing. But
never have I sacrificed a babe or seen the future in
smoke or danced naked 'round a fire. *(Beat. She smiles)*
Oui, but you like the thought of that, don't you?

(He turns, starts to leave)

VIRGINIE
Don't go.

JEAN
You've done what I paid you to do.

VIRGINIE
Oui, but...

JEAN
But what?

VIRGINIE
You know the loneliness, same as I. A little company…

JEAN
The townsfolk pay you to stuff their trophies. That would be company enough for me and more.

VIRGINIE
They come, they drop a dead thing at my feet and say "Make it look alive, make it look fierce", and I do. That isn't company; that's barter. It's been some time since a handsome man came to…talk.

(Long pause. JEAN has no idea what to say. Finally—)

JEAN
My arm hurts.

(Beat)

VIRGINIE
Sterling conversationalist, you are.

JEAN
What should I say? I've been mauled by a…creature and sewn up on a butcher's table. It bloody well hurts!

(Beat. She smiles. He laughs a little. She offers him some more wine)

JEAN
How much?

VIRGINIE
Free of charge. This time.

JEAN
Good enough. *(He takes it and drinks. He makes a face)*

VIRGINIE
Not the finest vintage, but we don't drink it for the
taste.

JEAN
Oui.

(He hands it back. She drinks)

VIRGINIE
Why have you not visited me before? We are the only
two out this far. That makes us perhaps neighbors.

JEAN
If I wanted friends, I'd…I don't want friends.

VIRGINIE
Never lonely? Not even once?

JEAN
I just don't see the sense in it. Even the best of them…
they open their mouths and I want to throttle them.

VIRGINIE
Even me?

JEAN
If this arm starts to turn? We'll see.

VIRGINIE
I think you're here because you wanted to meet me.

JEAN
Pfft.

VIRGINIE
A wound like that, you could've stitched up yourself.

JEAN
These hands weren't meant for thread and needle.

VIRGINIE
Maybe was your own dog that big you, and you thought
to yourself "Ah-ha! Now I have a reason to meet that
beautiful witch that lives up the way." How far from the
mark am I, hmm?

(Beat. He laughs and dons his coat)

JEAN
I thank you, Mem'selle.

(He starts to leave)

VIRGINIE
You cannot go out there!

JEAN
No?

VIRGINIE
The damned Beast might still be lurking about! Why
risk it?

JEAN
Risk is what makes life taste sweet.

VIRGINIE
Is my company so foul you'd rather face la Bete de
Gévaudan?

(Beat)

JEAN
Your company isn't foul. My soul is.

VIRGINIE
Fine! Go back to your little hovel and dream of gold
you'll never have!

JEAN
I shall.

VIRGINIE
What use have you for it? Will you buy a great maison to fill with no one?

JEAN
Mayhap.

VIRGINIE
If I were truly a witch, I'd look into the tea leaves and say "This is a man who will die alone and unmourned."

JEAN
I am staggered by your insight.

(He opens the door)

VIRGINIE
Watch your step, hunter. If the Beast is out there, then even odds you'll die before you see your hovel.

JEAN
You're a betting woman then?

(She shrugs. He reaches into his pocket and tosses her a coin. She catches it)

JEAN
That silver says I survive the night.

(She walks towards him, examining the coin)

VIRGINIE
All your life is worth? One silver?

JEAN
It'll buy my corpse a grave, if nothing else.

VIRGINIE
A grave? For you? I'll let your body rot and use this to buy my bread.

JEAN
I truly believe you would.

VIRGINIE
It was good to meet you, M'sieu Chastel, moments before your death.

JEAN
We shall see, Mem'selle. We shall see.

(He kisses her. She's shocked, but doesn't fight it)

VIRGINIE
I think mayhap that is why you came here tonight.

JEAN
Mayhap.

VIRGINIE
I should slap you.

JEAN
(Putting on his hat and smiling) You should.

(He exits. Lights fade)

SCENE TWO

(*A week later. VIRGINIE is washing the table. There's a knock on the door. She sighs*)

VIRGINIE
Patience, patience.

(*She throws the wet rag into a bucket, then opens the door while she's rolling up her sleeves. JEAN is there, two dead rabbits slung over his shoulder*)

VIRGINIE
Bon soir.

JEAN
Bon soir.

(*They stare at each other. He smiles*)

JEAN
It would seem you owe me a silver, mem'selle.

VIRGINIE
A week I waited for you to collect it. I was sure you were wolf scat by now. Come. (*She lets him in*)

JEAN
I felt so.

VIRGINIE
Oui?

JEAN
The wound began to burn. I was very sick.

VIRGINIE
You should've come sooner!

JEAN
I couldn't leave my damned bed but to roll over and retch!

VIRGINIE
Let me see it. *(She grabs his arm, rolls up the sleeve)* Looks better. Much better.

JEAN
Oui. The fever broke yesterday. The infection didn't set.

VIRGINIE
And now?

JEAN
Now what?

VIRGINIE
How do you feel?

(He tosses the two rabbits on the table)

JEAN
Well enough to hunt again.

VIRGINIE
You wish me to stuff these? *(She picks one up, trying to make it look menacing by raising its paws)* I can make

it ferocious, if you like.

(He laughs)

VIRGINIE
"Beware the deadly fanged rabbits of the woods!"

JEAN
Stuff it if you wish, but I have no need of trophies. Those are for your stewpot.

VIRGINIE
Gallant of you.

JEAN
Ha! Mayhap that's the first time I've heard that word and my name together.

VIRGINIE
Payment for the stitching?

JEAN
I believe I gave you more than enough of my coin.

(She shrugs)

JEAN
I am not incapable of gratitude.

VIRGINIE
Oh! Now that's a fancy thing.

(Beat)

JEAN
Most hate me.

VIRGINIE
Truth in that.

JEAN
The people of the province...they would like me

better as a corpse rotting in the earth. But you... helped me. I am grateful.

(She stares at him. She then grabs his shoulders and kisses him on the cheek)

VIRGINIE
Outcasts must care for outcasts, for who else would care for us?

JEAN
Truly.

VIRGINIE
Thank you for the meat. They'll make a fine meal.

JEAN
Will you use the bones? For your witchcraft?

(She smiles)

JEAN
I've heard tell that witches can cast bones to see the future.

VIRGINIE
And are you so sure I am a witch? Perhaps the towns-folk just say that to be rid of me.

JEAN
There's more to you than skinning knives and twine.

VIRGINIE
Mayhap.

JEAN
I cannot say for certain you're a witch, but I think there's something of old magic about you.

VIRGINIE
I like the way you flirt.

JEAN
I am not flirting.

VIRGINIE
Oh? Is that so?

(Beat. He's uncomfortable)

JEAN
Do what you will with the hares. *(He turns to leave)*

VIRGINIE
So bashful! Sit, sit, sit. *(She kicks a chair towards him)* You wish to know if I'm a witch? Even I do not know. What most call magic, I call herbcraft. But I cannot summon spirits or fly from my body. Old wives tales. And I am neither old, nor a wife.

JEAN
No husband then?

VIRGINIE
Once. He built this palace you stand in. We lay together as man and wife for before...

(Beat)

VIRGINIE
A tale for another time. *(Pours them both some wine, then clinks her cup against his)* To outcasts. *(She takes the rabbits to another table, begins to clean and chop them as they talk, her back to him)* I'm glad you lived.

JEAN
As am I.

VIRGINIE
Even as small a bite as that can go rotten.

JEAN
Mayhap.

VIRGINIE
You're tougher than tanned hide, you are.

JEAN
A life alone will do that. You know.

VIRGINIE
Oui. I know. *(She raises her cleaver and chops off the heads of the rabbits)* Gods, I love that sound. THUNK!

JEAN
You're good with a knife.

VIRGINIE
I'd have to be, eh? Cutting, gutting, skinning, cleaning, stitching...all I can do to make a living. Well, and sell a few weeds on the side.

JEAN
You do good work.

VIRGINIE
Flirt.

JEAN
I speak truth. I've never seen their equal.

(She picks up one of the animals, holds it lovingly)

VIRGINIE
I love my art, if I love anything at all. They are mine, each and every one. I shape them, I give them life again, after a fashion. It is a harder craft than most know.

JEAN
I couldn't do it.

VIRGINIE
No. You couldn't. I've never met another who can do what I do. They may be stitch and sawdust to you. But to me...my children. My own true friends. That

is why I love them.

JEAN
That bear is magnificent.

VIRGINIE
Ah! Old Gaspard! *(She pats the bear affectionately)*
My husband brought this great beast low. He was a
hunter, like you.

JEAN
No.

(Beat)

JEAN
A hunter, mayhap. But not like me. No one's like me.

VIRGINIE
As you say. My husband...Marcel...we'd been starv-
ing. A bad winter. You know how those are. We'd not
stored away enough, and...he got it into his fool head
to kill a bear.

JEAN
A bear? In winter? I thought you said he was a hunter.

VIRGINIE
I also said he was a fool. He was forever in those woods,
trying to find anything...the bigger, the better. And
the more time he spent out there...the woods change
a man. You know this.

(She looks to JEAN. He nods)

VIRGINIE
I do not know the reason. But there is something out
there, something that...

JEAN
It calls to you.

(Beat)

VIRGINIE
Yes.

JEAN
And to him, and to me. The quiet of it, the wild of it.
It reminds us what we really are.

*(Beat. That hits closer to home than VIRGINIE would
like)*

VIRGINIE
After almost a month, Marcel found a cave. And the
bear sleeping inside it. All my man could see was a
great pile of meat for our bellies and fur for our bed.
He took this very musket...*(She takes the musket off
the wall, points it)*...aimed it true, at the big, fat slum-
bering thing and...PFFFT. *(She mimes smoke coming
off the hammer)* Wet powder. So of course old Gaspard
here perked up his ears and woke. What should have
been an easy kill was now a great, slavering monster
as big as...well, as big as this! *(She slaps the bear's
belly)*

JEAN
How did Marcel kill it?

VIRGINIE
Well, and I had only his word for it, but he said he
tried to beat the thing with this damn musket. But
can you imagine braining a bear to death?

JEAN
No.

VIRGINIE
Well, after a few whacks, neither could Marcel.
So he took out the one weapon he had left. *(She*

takes a large hunting knife and plunges it into the table)
He took this and... *(She thrusts it upwards. She then
takes JEAN and brings him to the bear. She shows him
a spot under its jaw)* You see that? That scar there?
Marcel shoved his knife into old Gaspard's brain.
Dropped him then and there. Well, night had come
and he wasn't going to drag the great bulk all the
way home in the dark. So he used the bear...as
a bed! Ha! God's truth! Just curled up on top of
that shaggy hide and spent the night sleeping in
the bear's den! When morning broke, he tied it to
a sled and brought it back to me. We ate well for
a month and more on him. But we were careful in
cutting him, in gutting him...because Marcel bore
scars from that fight. A fight like that deserves a
trophy.

JEAN
Why "Gaspard?"

VIRGINIE
Hmmm?

JEAN
I'm certain the bear didn't tell you his name. So why
do you call him that?

VIRGINIE
Oh. *(Beat. She stares at the bear's face)* I don't know.
He just seems like a Gaspard, don't you think?

JEAN
I've never known a named bear.

VIRGINIE
Something about those jowls, I think. I don't know.
He's Gaspard because I say he's Gaspard. I have to call
him something if I...

(Beat)

JEAN
You talk to him.

VIRGINIE
No.

JEAN
Yes, you do.

VIRGINIE
Pffft.

JEAN
You're alone here...what? Days? Weeks? You found yourself talking to your little pets, and you gave them names.

VIRGINIE
That's the most foolish thing I've ever heard. (Beat. She looks at a stuffed owl) Don't you think so, Pierre?

(Beat. They laugh)

VIRGINIE
Laugh all you want, m'sieu. I prefer their company. Animals are easier than people.

JEAN
Even dead animals?

VIRGINIE
Especially dead animals! They eat no food, leave no droppings...perfect companions.

JEAN
There's many a woman would blanch to wake in a room with such beasts.

(She leans in, clinks his glass)

VIRGINIE
That must be why most women don't like me. Men neither, come to it.

(Beat. He kisses her. They fall into each other for a bit)

VIRGINIE
Well, not all men, it seems.

JEAN
I like how you smell.

VIRGINIE
Are you a hound then?

JEAN
Mayhap.

VIRGINIE
Yes, you're something...you understand the line between man and beast.

JEAN
I understand that there is no line.

VIRGINIE
Yes. Just so. (She breaks away) Is this why you're here?

JEAN
You talk too much.

VIRGINIE
Not that I'll begrudge a good roll. And I like a man who courts with a fresh kill. But...

JEAN
Stop. Talking.

(He grabs her, kisses her. She holds him back)

VIRGINIE
Tell me what you want, Chastel. And I'll tell you what
you can get.

JEAN
I thought what I wanted was clear.

VIRGINIE
There are those who tried to force their wants on me.
I showed them how good I was with a knife.

JEAN
I imagine you kept their gelded bits in a jar.

(She laughs)

VIRGINIE
You've not known me long, but you know me well.

JEAN
I mean to know you better.

VIRGINIE
And I mean to enjoy it...after you tell me the truth.

JEAN
You're maddening.

VIRGINIE
And more than a little mad. But humor the hostess.

(He rises, frustrated)

VIRGINIE
Don't scowl. You look like a gnarled old tree.

JEAN
You toy with me.

VIRGINIE
Hardly that. I simply guessed you wanted more from
me than my bed, and you're growling because of it.

JEAN
Bah!

VIRGINIE
So tell me. Tell me what you want, and if I like what
I hear, we'll dance this dance again.

(Beat. He stares at her)

JEAN
The Beast...it's not killed a soul since...

VIRGINIE
Since you shot it.

JEAN
Oui. And I was thinking...what if...that is, I shot it
squarely in the chest. It dropped. And...

VIRGINIE
No silver bullet, no death.

JEAN
Oui, if it were a Loup Garou...but what if it
wasn't?!

VIRGINIE
You said yourself it...

JEAN
The night was foggy! And, mayhap I'd had a nip before
I'd gone hunting.

VIRGINIE
So you think then...

JEAN
It's possible, no? That I killed it and simply...lost it.
If the beast loped off into the woods, I may never see
its corpse.

VIRGINIE
The crows may have picked it clean by now.

JEAN
And my hope of collecting three hundred livre gone
with it.

VIRGINIE
Unless...?

(Beat. He stares at her)

VIRGINIE
Methinks you're here because you have an "Unless."

JEAN
Three hundred livre would buy a one a new life...a
better life. And still have enough left for another.

VIRGINIE
I'm listening.

JEAN
I may not be loved hereabouts, but I am known. A
great hunter.

VIRGINIE
Some say, the best in all of Gévaudan.

JEAN
It would be no difficult thing for me to convince
these simpletons that I slew the beast.

VIRGINIE
But you have no beast to show them.

JEAN
Oui.

VIRGINIE
And that is what you want from me.

(Beat)

JEAN
Oui.

VIRGINIE
Ha! I knew it! Gods above, I knew it!

JEAN
What?

VIRGINIE
When you first came to me...I knew it was for more than stitches!

JEAN
Cherie...

VIRGINIE
Needed a reason to meet me, eh? To see my work with your own two eyes? Oh, you are a crafty beast, you are.

JEAN
I tell you, I was wolf bit. I needed help, and you...

VIRGINIE
Half.

JEAN
What?

VIRGINIE
Half your gold, fool. You may be the one to claim the prize, but I'm doing much of the work.

JEAN
Then you'll do it?

VIRGINIE
For a hundred fifty livres? I'd do that and worse!

JEAN
It's a crime. You understand that, Oui?

VIRGINIE
Oui.

JEAN
If Louis discovers we've swindled his reward, our
heads will likely be on the block.

VIRGINIE
IF he discovers, which he'll not. And IF he could
catch us, which he can't.

JEAN
Christ, woman. Do you fear anything?

(Beat)

VIRGINIE
One thing only.

JEAN
What's that then?

VIRGINIE
Not for you to know.

JEAN
Keep your mysteries. A wolf for a hundred fifty livres.
D'accord?

*(He spits in his hand, offers it. She considers it, then
shakes)*

VIRGINIE
D'accord. *(She begins to laugh)* Christ almighty, did you
think you'd have to seduce me to win me to your cause?

JEAN
A good hunter uses all his tools.

VIRGINIE
Hunting me, are you?

JEAN
Mayhap.

VIRGINIE
I think I like putting my foot in your snare, only to
leap out as you pull it tight.

JEAN
Now who flirts?

VIRGINIE
Ha! *(She looks around)* My best wolf is in my cellar. I
was changing out his eyes.

JEAN
Virginie…

VIRGINIE
He's a big one…eight stone easy. And a good pelt of
thick grey fur. His name is Lucien.

JEAN
He will not do.

VIRGINIE
You're welcome to look about my collection, but I
speak the truth. Lucien is by far my best wolf.

JEAN
You do not understand.

VIRGINIE
But if you pick another, don't tell him. He can be a
jealous one.

JEAN
I do not doubt the quality of your work, but any wolf
you have will not do.

VIRGINIE
Then why come to me? You want to take my biggest squirrel and say "Behold! The Beast of Gévaudan?"

JEAN
The Beast I shall present to Louis...it must be greater than any wolf, than any creature the people of France have ever seen.

(She stares at him, confused)

JEAN
Could a simple wolf had slaughtered over a hundred men and women...eluded the greatest hunters for three years? Even the King's own hunters? No, even if I brought in a thing as fierce as your Lucien, they would simply look at it and say "That? That cannot be the Beast! It is only a wolf!"

VIRGINIE
Hmmm...

JEAN
What I bring to the court...it must be beyond monstrous. A creature of the Devil himself. They must look at it and understand why they could not catch it. A man can hunt a wolf, but...

VIRGINIE
But only Jean Chastel can catch...The Beast.

(He smiles)

JEAN
Just so.

VIRGINIE
So what is your scheme, then? I think you'd not have walked through my door if you'd not thought it out.

JEAN
Perhaps I just wanted my silver.

(She takes a silver from her pocket & tosses it to him. He catches it)

VIRGINIE
You have it. Now tell me.

(He slowly walks to her)

JEAN
I will bring you something.

VIRGINIE
A gift?

JEAN
An animal, the likes of which you've never seen.

VIRGINIE
I've seen many things.

JEAN
I'll surprise you yet. *(He stands behind her, smells her hair)*

VIRGINIE
And where did you find this...?

(He kisses her neck. She smiles)

JEAN
You talk too much.

VIRGINIE
I do at that. *(She turns around, kisses him)* Do not think me your wife.

JEAN
Why would I want to do that?

VIRGINIE
Many think a man's to own a woman.

JEAN
I not that sort.

VIRGINIE
Nor am I.

(They kiss. VIRGINIE sweeps off the table as they fall upon it. Lights change)

SCENE THREE

(A week later. VIRGINIE stokes the fire. She routinely looks at the door. After a bit, it swings open as JEAN shoulders his way in)

VIRGINIE
You used to knock.

JEAN
I'll need help.

VIRGINIE
A gentleman knocks.

JEAN
Gentlemen wear powdered wigs and piss in golden pots. Will you help me or not?

VIRGINIE
In golden pots? Truly?

JEAN
I don't know! Just clear the damn table!

(She sweeps the table clear as JEAN heads back outside. He returns dragging in something in a huge sack. From his effort, it's clear the contents are very heavy)

VIRGINIE
Good Christ...

JEAN
A moment...

VIRGINIE
What is...?

JEAN
...come on, you great bastard...

(With a great heave, he drags the thing to the table)

VIRGINIE
You see? You didn't need my help.

JEAN
Not for that. To get it on the table. Come.

(She just stares at the thing)

JEAN
Now!

VIRGINIE
Yes, yes, yes.

(She leans down, grabs one end of the sack as JEAN grabs the other)

JEAN
And...lift!

(The two strain to get the sack onto the table. With some effort, they succeed)

VIRGINIE
Satan's beard...did you bring me a bag of bricks?!

JEAN
My back...

VIRGINIE
What is this thing?

JEAN
Why don't you take a look?

(She places a hand on the sack, but hesitates)

JEAN
Scared?

VIRGINIE
No.

JEAN
You are.

VIRGINIE
Pffft.

JEAN
You think perhaps a hellhound is in there? A demon?

VIRGINIE
How could I know?

JEAN
Only one way.

(Beat. She opens the bag and looks in. She covers her mouth and backs away)

VIRGINIE
Merde!

JEAN
Impressive, non?

VIRGINIE
What...what is it?

JEAN
Never seen its like, I'd wager.

VIRGINIE
I've seen many things. More than you can imagine.
But I've never seen...that.

JEAN
Few in France have.

VIRGINIE
Where did you...?

JEAN
Chantilly.

VIRGINIE
Non!

JEAN
Oui.

VIRGINIE
You went all the way to Chantilly?!

JEAN
Oui.

VIRGINIE
Gone for a week...that explains why.

JEAN
Have you ever been there?

VIRGINIE
I've never been anywhere.

JEAN
Wonderful sights there. Beautiful gardens, a grand
fountain...and a menagerie. *(He slaps the thing in the
bag)* A menagerie with one less beast.

VIRGINIE
You didn't!

JEAN
I am Jean Chastel...and I am the greatest hunter in
France. I can find anything!

VIRGINIE
This is some devil from another land then?

JEAN
Oh yes. It is called la hyène. From Africa, of all places.

VIRGINIE
As far as that?

JEAN
As far as that.

VIRGINIE
The world is a wondrous place.

JEAN
All the more wondrous for something like this. Savage,
brutal, perfect.

VIRGINIE
The teeth on it...

JEAN
There were bones in its cage. Backbones. Bitten
straight through.

VIRGINIE
No beast could do that.

JEAN
This one can. Snap right through it and sup on the marrow within. *(He goes to the sack)* This fellow died two days past. Poisoned. When they threw it onto the offal pile, I crept in and took it.

VIRGINIE
Poisoned?

JEAN
Oui.

VIRGINIE
By you, I assume?

JEAN
I'd have rather waited for it to die of age, but c'est la vie. *(He opens the sack, stares at it)* This is nature, ma chere. Utterly pure, utterly fierce. It cares not for man's laws or social contracts. It breeds, it hunts, and it runs free.

VIRGINIE
You may hate men, but you love this creature.

JEAN
I admire it. It's a perfect killer. We are kin.

VIRGINIE
Is that so?

JEAN
What is a human but a weak heart and a cluttered mind? Pathetic. But out here...in the wild...we become what we are meant to be. You said before that the woods change a man? *(He grabs the thing in the sack)* THIS is what it changes us into.

VIRGINIE
I may be a little in love with you, Chastel. *(She kisses*

him deeply, then studies the thing in the bag) This is
going to take some time. Bigger than a wolf by half.

JEAN
How long?

VIRGINIE
If I work on nothing else? A week.

JEAN
A week?!

VIRGINIE
I'm not a seamstress, and this isn't lace and felt! Do
you have any concept how hard it is to stitch hide?
To reset and sculpt bone?

JEAN
...no...

VIRGINIE
Say again?

JEAN
I do not know how to do what you do!

VIRGINIE
And that's god's truth. There is an art to this. My art,
my pride and joy!

JEAN
I'm aware. That's why I'm here with you.

(She smiles)

VIRGINIE
The only reason?

JEAN
I can think of no other.

VIRGINIE
I'm certain. *(She kisses him)* That thing is all jaws and
teeth.

JEAN
Why I chose it. There were other creatures there...
great cats, even a lizard as long as I am tall!

VIRGINIE
Truth?

JEAN Jaws like this! *(He opens his arms to indicate
huge jaws)* I thought it was a dragon, but with no wings!

VIRGINIE
Ha!

JEAN
It let out this bellow...this roar...it sounded like the
souls of the damned.

VIRGINIE
I've not had the pleasure of hearing a damned soul.

JEAN
You say that, but I don't believe it.

VIRGINIE
You're smarter than you look, Chastel. *(She looks at
the thing in the sack)*

JEAN
I saw this beast before. Years ago, before it died. The
sound it made...

VIRGINIE
Oh?

JEAN
It had to be heard to be believed.

VIRGINIE
Show me!

JEAN
I cannot.

VIRGINIE
Please! Oh please!

JEAN
No.

VIRGINIE
I ask so little of you.

(Beat. He sighs, then tries to imitate the barking laugh
of a hyena. VIRGINIE laughs)

VIRGINIE
What in all the hells was that?

JEAN
That was the sound it made!

VIRGINIE
No.

JEAN
Yes! It...it...

VIRGINIE
It laughed?

JEAN
It was like a laugh, but...I have hunted every creature
that walks in France, and not felt a whit of fear. But
that sound...the sound that thing made? That will
stay with me the rest of my life.

VIRGINIE
When I was a child, my mother said there were no

monsters but the ones called men. And now you show
me this. A true monster. Thank you.

JEAN
Most wouldn't consider that a gift.

VIRGINIE
Most are fools then.

(She kisses him. They look at it again)

JEAN
Make it monstrous. A thing from the depths of Hell.

VIRGINIE
That shouldn't be over-hard.

JEAN
When I unveil it at court, I want the women to faint.
(Beat. He senses a mood change) What?

VIRGINIE
I should be there too.

JEAN
No. We discussed this.

VIRGINIE
I am the artist! You're just...!

JEAN
I am the man who killed the Beast of Gévaudan. If
you are there, questions may be asked. "Why bring
the woods witch? Are they both in league with the
Devil?"

VIRGINIE
I will stay hidden!

JEAN
We can take no chances! None! That fat skinflint of

a King would take any opportunity to deny me...to deny US our just reward.

VIRGINIE
Hardly just.

JEAN
Two weeks now, and the Beast has killed no one! It is dead and gone!

VIRGINIE
And what if it's not? What if it returns on the next full moon and kills more while you're at the palace?! They'll know you for a liar and...

JEAN
I escaped Chantilly with this carcass on my back. I can escape that fop.

VIRGINIE
And lead his guards back to me?

JEAN
(*Taking her hand*) We'll flee. We'll run to the woods. None know them better than us.

VIRGINIE
It's a great risk. Let me take it with you.

JEAN
No.

VIRGINIE
It is not right! I...

JEAN
When I left you, we were in agreement. Now I return to this?

(*Beat*)

VIRGINIE
Do not betray me, Chastel. That is all I ask. Do not betray me.

JEAN
I'll not. You have my word.

VIRGINIE
I don't know you well enough to trust your word.

JEAN
What can I give you, eh? What would you take on loan as a sign of good faith? I have nothing!

(She stares at him, thinking)

VIRGINIE
We will make a pact.

JEAN
I thought we already had.

VIRGINIE
A blood pact. Binding us to this deed we do.

JEAN
I thought you said you were not a witch.

VIRGINIE
I also said I know a thing about a thing.

(He backs away from her)

VIRGINIE
If you mean to play me fair, then you've nothing to worry about.

JEAN
I don't trust sorcery.

VIRGINIE
It is an old science, nothing more. Unless...are you

afraid now?

JEAN
I fear nothing!

VIRGINIE
Then you surely won't fear a little blood, and a little...something else. *(Beat)* This is the bridge we must cross, chere. Whatever fondness we have, I trust you no more than you trust me. But we two mean to cheat the King of France. This is no small thing.

(Beat)

JEAN
I do not like this.

VIRGINIE
Do you like gold?

(Beat. He offers his hand)

JEAN
Do as you will.

VIRGINIE
That's my brave man. *(She takes a large knife from the table, and a pouch from the cabinet)* This will hurt.

JEAN
Life hurts.

(She quickly cuts his hand. He winces, but doesn't cry out)

VIRGINIE
This will hurt more.

(She pours powder from the pouch onto his hand. This time, he snarls in pain)

JEAN
Damnation! What was...?

(She takes the knife, cutting her own palm without even a wince. She then pours the powder on her own hand and grabs his, pressing their cuts together)

VIRGINIE
Sanguis meus, tuum est enim sanguis meus.

JEAN
Let me go!

VIRGINIE
Per herbam tenemur.

JEAN
Stop!

VIRGINIE
Lupus est vinculum!

(She lets him go. He staggers, suddenly feeling week)

VIRGINIE
The sickness will pass quickly.

JEAN
What...was in that powder?

VIRGINIE
Old things.

(He sits against the wall, rubbing his eyes)

JEAN
It's like...drinking a cask of wine...all in one swallow.

VIRGINIE
We are bound now, by what we mean to do. You will not betray me. *(She goes to him, taking his face in her hands)* Look at me. This is what passes for trust to the likes of us. So long as you play me fair, all will be well.

JEAN
And if I don't?

(Beat)

VIRGINIE
You will. *(She helps him back to his feet, then slaps him hard when he's standing)*

JEAN
Dammit!

VIRGINIE
Better?

(He rubs his eyes)

JEAN
Better. Give me some damn water.

(She does so. He drinks & splashes some on his face)

JEAN
I've never been spelled before.

VIRGINIE
That was only a little one.

JEAN
I knew you were a witch.

VIRGINIE
Does putting a name on what I am make me more intriguing or less?

JEAN
It simply makes you...you.

VIRGINIE
I am already me. I need no name for it then. *(She binds his hand)* You can say the Beast did this to you

as you fought. Add to the legend of Jean Chastel.

JEAN
Mayhap I will.

VIRGINIE
How did you live so long? It seems I'm always bandaging you.

JEAN
You're the one who cut me, woman!

VIRGINIE
Oh, that's right. Well, we've done worse, and will do worse yet. *(She kisses his bound palm)* There. To help it heal.

JEAN
You just like the taste of my blood.

VIRGINIE
Ha! That may be. *(She walks back to the thing in the sack)* I will work so many wonders on this thing.

JEAN
I'm relying on that.

VIRGINIE
You will have to tell me.

JEAN
Tell you what?

VIRGINIE
If any running screaming when they see it. That is my dearest wish.

JEAN
Ma cherie, I can all but promise it. *(He walks to her, both staring at it)* This is our salvation.

VIRGINIE
Oui.

JEAN
When you have created your masterpiece, when I
have presented it to the King...all we've ever wanted
will be ours.

VIRGINIE
A strange idea, that.

JEAN
Why?

VIRGINIE
People like you and I...we weren't meant to have. We
were meant to live on the scraps of others.

JEAN
Where is that written?

VIRGINIE
It has ever been thus.

JEAN
To hell with that. We've lived on scraps for too long.
We've been spit on by those who have no idea what
it means to truly live. You and I? We know this world.
We ARE this world! Clawed and fanged and alive,
with no worry for laws or kindness or trappings of
civility!

VIRGINIE
For a wildman, you're working very hard for Louis'
gold.

JEAN
If I could live solely on trading pelts, I would. But
gold...I may hate it, but I know it solves problems.

VIRGINIE
I would disagree, but you've seen the splendor I live in.

JEAN
Not for long. Soon, I will buy us a...

VIRGINIE
Us? You'll buy "us" what exactly?

JEAN
I misspoke.

VIRGINIE
And you said you didn't mate for life.

JEAN
You are not my mate! You are my...

VIRGINIE
Your witch?

JEAN
My friend.

(Beat. She smiles)

VIRGINIE
Your friend that you roll with from time to time.

JEAN
Is there a better sort of friendship?

VIRGINIE
None that I know.

(They kiss)

JEAN
Tell me.

VIRGINIE
Tell you what?

JEAN
What you're going to do. To our Beast.

VIRGINIE
I could tell you…or I could show you. Grab that.

(She points to a tool on the wall. He hands it to her)

JEAN
What's it for?

VIRGINIE
I'll crack open its jaws, then expand them with wire and reset them.

JEAN
That will be a sight to see.

VIRGINIE
When I'm done, it will look as though it could swallow a carriage wheel.

JEAN
Perfect.

(She strokes the bag as though petting a dog)

VIRGINIE
It will be. Perfect. My greatest creation. The monster I made.

JEAN
La loup garou.

VIRGINIE
The Beast of Gévaudan. I mean to make a believer out of any who look upon it.

JEAN
Even you?

VIRGINIE
We shall see. *(She takes his hand)* You, the hunter who
laid it low. Me, the witch who gave it life.

JEAN
What a pair we make.

VIRGINIE
Would you like to watch? To see how a beast is made?

*(Beat. JEAN walks up behind her, putting his arms
around her)*

JEAN
Very much.

*(She grabs a pair of large knives from the table. She
peels back some of the bag so that she can see the creature, although the audience cannot)*

JEAN
Do you know where to begin?

VIRGINIE
Oh yes. I know a thing about a thing.

*(She thrusts in the knife and begins to cut. Blood sprays
out. Lights fade)*

Scene Four

(Lights up. JEAN is pacing about the room, clearly excited and anxious. VIRGINIE is working on something in another room, speaking through the door. It is a week later)

VIRGINIE
Stomp, stomp, stomp. Are you a good soldier, off to war?

JEAN
I want to see it.

VIRGINIE
You're not the first to say that to me.

JEAN
You said a week! It has been a week!

VIRGINIE
Oui, and it is near ready!

JEAN
"Near?!" What is "near?!"

VIRGINIE
Enough whining from you.

JEAN
I've already spread word of my fight with the beast! I
said that I killed it!

VIRGINIE
That was your choice.

JEAN
I needed the legend to begin before I set off to the
King's!

VIRGINIE
Also your choice.

JEAN
BAH! You don't understand.

VIRGINIE
I understand well enough. I just don't care.

JEAN
Bah!

VIRGINIE
Yours was to kill the Beast and claim the prize. Mine
was to make that very beast.

JEAN
Are you finished or are you not?!

(She re-enters the room)

VIRGINIE
I am.

*(He moves quickly towards the other room. VIRGINIE
intercepts him)*

VIRGINIE
Hold.

JEAN
I've waited enough!

VIRGINIE
And you'll wait a moment longer yet.

JEAN
Think you that?

VIRGINIE
(Drawing a large carving knife) I think that, and more.

(Beat. They stare at each other. JEAN smiles, begins to laugh. She joins in)

JEAN
We're a strange pair, are we not?

VIRGINIE
Oui, monsieur. But I like us that way.

JEAN
As do I.

(She puts the knife to his throat, then leans in and kisses him)

VIRGINIE
A bit of risk makes the kisses sweeter.

JEAN
Do I complain?

VIRGINIE
Often, yes.

JEAN
How you've endured me, I'll never know.

VIRGINIE
What is a wolf without some growling, non?

(He growls at her. She laughs)

JEAN
The waiting has grown wearisome, ma cherie.

VIRGINIE
I told you before; I am an artist. The painter does not
unveil the canvas until the paint is dry.

JEAN
It best be dry, woman. I have brought my wagon, and
leave for Versailles this day.

VIRGINIE
I know, I know. *(She walks to the door, stops)* Christ
but I'm nervous.

JEAN
You? You of all people?

VIRGINIE
I've never made beasts for aught but peasants. But
this...this will go before a King.

JEAN
Louis is a man like any other. And a bigger fool than
many I know. He should be honored to be in the
presence of your miracles.

(Beat. VIRGINIE smiles)

VIRGINIE
Your lips drip honey when you wish them to.

JEAN
Speaking the truth prettily doesn't make it a lie.

(She turns, stares at him)

JEAN
What is it?

VIRGINIE
I love you a bit, Chastel. Mayhap more than a bit even.

JEAN
Truly?

VIRGINIE
Oui.

(He says nothing)

VIRGINIE
Do you not feel for me? Even a little?

(Beat)

JEAN
None have ever said it to me before. Not and meant it.

VIRGINIE
Never, in all your life?

JEAN
I'm glad it was you.

(He takes her hand, kisses her)

VIRGINIE
I knew you loved me a little.

JEAN
Just another secret to add to the pile.

(She stares into the room, takes a deep breath)

VIRGINIE
You're ready then?

JEAN
I am.

VIRGINIE
Monsieur Chastel, I give you...the Beast of Gévaudan!

(She pulls a large, covered creature into the room. She then pulls the sheet off the beast. It is a large stuffed hyena, posed to be particularly terrifying. JEAN gasps, takes a step backwards)

JEAN
Baise-moi!

VIRGINIE
Then you approve?

(He nods, utterly stunned by what he's looking at. He walks a circle around it)

JEAN
I cannot see the old corpse I had slung over my back.

VIRGINIE
Good.

JEAN
This...no demon in hell could match this.

VIRGINIE
I am proud most of the eyes and the mouth.

JEAN
Yes...

VIRGINIE
Do you see what I did?

(He shakes his head)

VIRGINIE
The glass eyes I used...not a wolves.

(He stares at the beast's face)

JEAN
A man.

VIRGINIE
Oui.

JEAN
You gave it a man's eyes.

VIRGINIE
It is a loup-garou, non? Tho' we see the beast, some
hint of the man should be there as well.

JEAN
It is us in reverse.

VIRGINIE
Oui. We walk as men walk, live as men live, and only
show the beast but a little.

JEAN
Exquisite.

VIRGINIE
Then you like it?

JEAN
What I feel is…something more.

VIRGINIE
I love all my little children, but this? This is my greatest work. Never have I been so proud.

JEAN
Remarkable.

*(His hands have drifted towards its mouth. As he touches
the teach, VIRGINIE snarls loudly. JEAN falls back,
startled. VIRGINIE laughs)*

VIRGINIE
Forgive me, chere. I could not help myself.

JEAN
I damn near pissed myself.

VIRGINIE
Hardly a way to appear before your liege.

JEAN
Three hundred livre will buy many new pants.

VIRGINIE
One hundred fifty livre, monsieur.

JEAN
Yes. Of course.

VIRGINIE
You'll not cheat me.

JEAN
I said I won't and I won't.

VIRGINIE
What you say doesn't matter. I've hexed you. You'll
hold true or...

JEAN
Or what, cherie? You've been mum on that end.

(She takes his hand)

VIRGINIE
Hold true, and never find out. *(She kisses him deeply)*
Go now. Take our pet to his new master, and keep
your prick out of those Verailles whores.

JEAN
You don't wear jealousy well.

VIRGINIE
Pfft! I'm not jealous! I just don't want you to catch
something vile. I can cure many things, but not all
things.

JEAN
As you say.

*(He walks towards the beast, but she keeps hold of his
hand. He turns to stare at her)*

JEAN
What is it?

VIRGINIE
Come back to me.

JEAN
Virginie, I...

VIRGINIE
Just...come back to me.

(He comes back to her, embraces her)

JEAN
I will, ma petite. I will.

(Lights fade)

Scene Five

(A few days later. A knock at VIRGINIE'S door. No response. Louder knocking. VIRGINIE enters in, groggy and a bit hung over)

VIRGINIE
A minute!

(She dunks her head in a water bowl, soaking her face and hair. She shakes herself out, then opens the door. JEAN stands there)

VIRGINIE
Jean! *(She hugs him. He hugs her back. She pushes him inside)* Inside already, you great fool!

JEAN
There are the sweet words I've missed.

VIRGINIE
A day early! I'd not expected you til tomorrow.

JEAN
I know what "a day early" means, cherie.

(They kiss)

VIRGINIE
And?

JEAN
And what?

VIRGINIE
Don't play coy with me, oaf. You know damn well
what I'm asking.

*(JEAN is about to speak, then reaches into his pack. He
takes out a sack of coins and tosses it to VIRGINIE.
She's taken aback by its weight)*

VIRGINIE
Mon dieu! Heavy!

JEAN
One hundred fifty livres is not a feather pillow.

VIRGINIE
The whole sum?! The old skinflint paid the whole
sum!?

JEAN
Count it out, if you'd like.

VIRGINIE
No need. I trust you.

*(Beat. She quickly sits at a table and starts to count the
coins)*

VIRGINIE
I've never seen so much in all my life.

JEAN
Like as not, you never will again.

VIRGINIE
Once is enough. Once is more than most get.

JEAN
Truly.

(She kicks a chair towards him)

JEAN
Ay!

VIRGINIE
Sit! Sit sit sit! Tell me everything.

JEAN
I do not know everything. How could I tell you everything if...?

VIRGINIE
Careful, Chastel. You're growing a sense of humor.

JEAN
What do you want to know?

VIRGINIE
Tell me of the palace.

JEAN
You cannot imagine. The chandeliers, the tapestries... I never understood why a man would hang painted cloth on walls, but then I saw them...some of them taller than this room!

VIRGINIE
Non!

JEAN
C'est vrais! And not just tapestries...heads! Great heads of boars and stags and bears...did you know that it was once a hunting lodge?

VIRGINIE
Truly?

JEAN
Oui. That's what Louis' father built it for! You'd not see it now, though. All red walls and grand staircases and…you could've fit this entire shack into the ballroom five times over!

VIRGINIE
It's not that small!

JEAN
Non, but the ballroom is that big!

VIRGINIE
You lie!

JEAN
May God strike me dead! He must have an entire village of servants, just to keep the place clean!

VIRGINIE
Did he give you the run of the place?

JEAN
Non, they tried to take me straight to the throne room, but I couldn't help but look about. Will I ever see le Château de Versailles again? I doubt it.

(She rises, crosses away)

JEAN
What?

VIRGINIE
You sulk for only seeing it once, when you know I will never see it at all.

JEAN
I didn't mean that.

VIRGINIE
All the same, that's what I heard.

JEAN
Christ, woman. Must we go over this again?

(She says nothing. He goes to her, putting his hands on her shoulders)

JEAN
They screamed.

(Beat)

JEAN
We put the beast on a cart, threw a sheet over it, and rolled it in. When I uncovered it, they screamed.

(Beat)

VIRGINIE
Truly?

JEAN
(Kissing her shoulder, her neck) I was certain you could hear them all the way out here.

(She smiles)

JEAN
Louis said, "This creature can only have come from the depths of Hell." *(He turns her around so she faces him)* I could not have done this without you.

VIRGINIE
I know. But I hate it.

JEAN
Porquoi?

VIRGINIE
You have to ask?! It was my work, Jean! MINE!

JEAN
We got our gold!

VIRGINIE
Aye, but only one of us got the glory.

JEAN
Had you been there, had Louis understood the truth
of it, we'd have gotten nothing at all.

VIRGINIE
I know that! You think I do not know that?! I
just…CHRIST! *(She hurls the bucket to the ground)*
Do you never rage against the…unfairness of it
all? No, of course not. Look at you…Jean Chastel,
killer of the Beast, greatest hunter in all of…

JEAN
You think I do not know unfairness, woman?! I am an
outcast…I am filth! Spat on by others, hated, alone…

VIRGINIE
Because you choose to be. *(Beat)* A man like you,
who can hunt and trap…you could make a place for
yourself in this world. You are an outcast because you
choose to be. But what of me, Chastel? What place is
there for a widow, a heretic who makes monsters and
dances under the moon? Gods, do NOT speak to me
of unfairness.

JEAN
Few are those who would weep for a woman holding
one hundred fifty livres in her hand.

VIRGINIE
Because the world is peopled with fools. *(She sits)*
When I was a girl…no more than this big…I dreamed
of something, anything beyond these woods. For

what child doesn't dream of a grand life? This...
(She motions to the room)...never did I dream of this.
Yet here I am.

JEAN
Here you are. *(He takes the coins, kneels to her and
puts them in her hands)* This world is naught but
cruelty and hardship, cherie. The destitute...we
simply see it more clearly, but do not doubt that all
that live suffer. We struggle against it all the same.
Those that can take from those that cannot. They
toss us their gnawed bones like we're dogs. But the
rarest thing of all, rarer than pearls from the sea, is
when the dogs rise up and steal from the master's
table. This...*(He shakes the bag of coins)*...is not an
end to suffering. But by whatever god you pray to,
this does make the suffering easier to bear.

VIRGINIE
I deserve more than pilfered gold.

JEAN
So do many. They'll never have what you have now.
Can you take no comfort in that?

(Beat. She examines the pouch)

VIRGINIE
Mayhap.

JEAN
That's my love. *(He kisses her)*

VIRGINIE
You're not without surprises.

JEAN
There's truth in that.

VIRGINIE
I imagine if I didn't love you a little, I'd have gutted you like a fish by now.

JEAN
Make me a promise.

VIRGINIE
Not to gut you?

JEAN
Not to do anything, say anything...foolish.

VIRGINIE
You do not trust me?

JEAN
No. I don't.

(Beat)

VIRGINIE
Probably why you've lived so long.

JEAN
We're walking through dangerous woods, cherie. And there are traps all about us. A single misstep, and we are caught. And if we are caught...

VIRGINIE
We are killed.

JEAN
Oui. That is why we must be smart, must be careful, and must be in accord.

VIRGINIE
I know.

JEAN
You made me make a pact. Hexed me should I break

it. Is it so startling that I'd want the same?

VIRGINIE
You mean to cast a spell on me, Chastel?

JEAN
Have I not already?

(She laughs. He smiles)

JEAN
You feel cheated, that I left you here and went to Versailles alone. So be it. Feel cheated. But by Christ, do not let your pride put our heads on the block. You hear me?

VIRGINIE
I've always heard you.

JEAN
You'll do it then? You'll speak not a word of this?

VIRGINIE
People may talk when I buy my first tapestry.

JEAN
You're smarter than that. You'll buy what you want, but far from town, where no one's heard of you.

VIRGINIE
Know me so well?

JEAN
Mayhap I do.

VIRGINIE
I half expect you to buy yourself a fine new home and fine new clothes.

JEAN
I may at that. The people of Gévaudan know I've

claimed my prize. If I don't spend it, they'll ask questions.

VIRGINIE
And there, the unfairness of the world rears its ugly head again. What good is all this if I cannot spend it!?

JEAN
You can, and you will. You need only be smart about it.

VIRGINIE
Do not name me a fool, Chastel.

JEAN
I've not, nor would I ever. But I'll have your word that you'll say nothing that will put us at risk.

VIRGINIE
Or what?

(Beat)

VIRGINIE
If I do not give you my word, what will you do, hmm?

(They are now face to face, standing very close)

JEAN
Why find out?

(They stare at each other for a bit, then start laughing)

VIRGINIE
Well enough, you great lout. I'll hold my tongue. But don't flaunt your fancy new clothes around me.

JEAN
A shame. I meant to buy a bejeweled codpiece.

(She laughs)

VIRGINIE
There's a picture.

JEAN
Have we fought enough then? I've ridden long and
far, I stink of the road, and we're both wearing too
many clothes.

VIRGINIE
You could've been a poet.

(They start walking to another room)

VIRGINIE
Think it's so easy to get under my skirts?

JEAN
What will happen, will happen.

VIRGINIE
Gods, you're tiresome.

*(She pushes him into the room as she begins to disrobe.
Lights fade)*

ACT II

Scene Six

(Lights rise. A few nights later. VIRGINIE opens her window. The sounds of the night pour in, as does the light of the setting sun. A candle is burning inside a bowl. She stares at it for a bit, then blows it out. After a bit, JEAN is heard singing outside. He knocks at the door. VIRGINIE stares at it, fingering a knife. Finally, she opens the door. JEAN is standing there in nicer clothes, clearly drunk)

JEAN
Bon nuit.

(Beat. He belches)

VIRGINIE
You stink.

JEAN
C'est impossible! I bathed today! Bathed, cherie! Not in the stream, in a damned bath! And cologne!

VIRGINIE
You smell like a Paris whore.

JEAN
You should've been there. HA! You should've been
IN there, with me...

(He staggers in. She closes the door behind him)

JEAN
Virginie...mon dieu! I was at Le Pannier...you know
it? A fine tavern in....

VIRGINIE
I know it.

JEAN
They cheered for me, Virginie. Cheered! "Jean
Chastel, slayer of the beast! Hero of Gévaudan!" I
didn't buy a single cup!

VIRGINIE
I'm certain.

JEAN
Every time I turned, someone filled my glass! And
all of them shouted "Tell the tale, Chastel! Tell the
tale!" And I did! HA! God strike me down as a liar
if I didn't!

VIRGINIE
I'm certain.

JEAN
I must've told it twenty times if it was one! How
I stalked the creature...a thing that seemed a wolf,
but walked upright, like a man! It evaded every trap,
I said. As cunning as it was ferocious! A day and a
night, I crept through the forest, finding signs of the
beast but never the beast itself! And then finally, I
knew!

VIRGINIE
Oh yes? Just what did you know?

JEAN
The reason I couldn't find it...it was hunting me!
I thought it was ahead of me, but it was behind!!
And so, I spun, musket at the ready! And there
it was....taller than I, with glowing red eyes and
fangs dripping blood! I all but froze. That's what
I told them, that I all but froze...unable to tear
myself away from those glowing eyes...and then,
it leaped! Well, in that very second, I regained my
wits and fired! *(He claps his hands loudly)* They'd all
gasp and I'd say "I knew what I was hunting, for
am I not Jean Chastel?" I'd not loaded common
shot into my musket, no. What pierced the heart
of the Beast was a silver ball, blessed by a priest.
It stared at me, shocked, knowing that its long life
was ending. And with a final howl to the moon, it
dropped. Oh, ma cherie, how they cheered! And if
any doubted, and those were few indeed, I said to
them, I said "Take your doubts to Marseilles! See
the creature there!"

*(He laughs loudly, oblivious to VIRGINIE's anger.
Finally —)*

VIRGINIE
He didn't.

JEAN
What's that?

VIRGINIE
He didn't strike you down.

JEAN
Who?

VIRGINIE
God. You said "God strike me down as a liar," yet
here you are.

JEAN
(Laughing again) Come now. You're not fool enough
to believe God punishes the false. Or that He even
exists at all!

VIRGINIE
You've not the first idea what I believe in.

(Beat)

JEAN
You're angry.

VIRGINIE
I am.

JEAN
I know, I know. You told me not to wear my new
finery around you, but how could I not? *(He stands,
showing off his coat)* Do I not cut a fine figure in
this?

VIRGINIE
I'm of a mind to cut you gob to gullet.

JEAN
Christ, but you're in a mood.

VIRGINIE
Why?

JEAN
How the hell should I know? You're half-mad sometimes.

VIRGINIE
WHY DID YOU LIE?!

(Beat)

JEAN
It was a lie we agreed upon. I couldn't tell them I took a trussed up African creature to...

(She is on him suddenly, a knife to his throat)

JEAN
CHRIST!

VIRGINIE
Not that, you drunken wretch! You told them you did it!

JEAN
Of course I did! We agreed that...

VIRGINIE
NO! You told them you stuffed the beast, that the creature in Louis' hall was made by you!

(Beat)

JEAN
I...

VIRGINIE
Lie to me, Chastel, and I will cut out your heart.

(Beat)

JEAN
If you wish me to speak, you'll need to lower your knife. *(She does so)* Christ, but that will sober a man fast.

VIRGINIE
A man came in today, looking to have me stuff his old dead dog. He walked about, admiring my work, and then...do you know what he said to me?

JEAN
Non.

VIRGINIE
"You do good work, tho' I hear Jean Chastel's is
better." I went breathless. The fellow told me a tale
of the great hunter of Gévaudan, the man who killed
the bloody Beast. I said "Oui, killed the beast. But
surely another must have prepared it for the King!"
"Non, non, ma petite!" he said. "I heard the tale
from Chastel's own lips! Two days he spent setting
the beast, stitching it up and making it fierce, before
he brought it to Versailles."

(Beat)

VIRGINIE
What say you to this, eh? Will you try to wiggle
your way free, serpent? Use that forked tongue of
yours?

JEAN
You do not understand.

VIRGINIE
Oh, I understand. I understand that every word that
slips from your lips isn't worth the dirt on my boots!

JEAN
Virginie, put the knife down and...

VIRGINIE
I took you to my bed! I trusted you! Devil's beard,
I gave myself to you and...

(Beat. Her rage starts to turn to sorrow)

VIRGINIE
...I loved you, Jean.

JEAN
I know, cherie. I know. But you left me no choice.

(She stares at him, shocked)

JEAN
The way you were speaking…I know you could not have kept our secret.

VIRGINIE
I could! I would have!

JEAN
And I think you believe it, but your pride…your pride would never have let you stay silent. You couldn't be happy just with your coin. You wanted more.

VIRGINIE
Had I said anything? No!

JEAN
It was only a matter of time. A casual remark here, a muttered complaint to the wrong ear, and all we had done would be undone. I couldn't allow that.

VIRGINIE
Then why not kill me, great hunter?

JEAN
You know why. *(Beat)* I hate damn near every soul walking this miserable earth. But not you. You, I love.

VIRGINIE
And this is how you show it?!

JEAN
This is how I protect you, and everything we've done.

VIRGINIE
Liar!

JEAN
I do love you, truly. But you have seen how wild you
can be. Now, even if you were to tell the truth of
what you've done, of your part in all this…who will
believe you, hmm? Who will believe some woman's
story over that of Gévaudan's hero and savior?

VIRGINIE
It's not fair!

JEAN
No, it is not. But it is what is best.

*(In a fury, VIRGINIE attacks JEAN. She slashes at
him wildly with the knife)*

JEAN
Stop!

(She snarls, tries to stab him. He grabs her arm)

JEAN
This is why! You cannot control your…

(She rakes her fingers down his face. He cries out)

JEAN
Merde!

VIRGINIE
Less pretty now, you pig.

(She slashes again, catching his arm. He backs away)

VIRGINIE
It was my work! My own! The greatest thing ever I
made, and you stole it from me!

(She stabs downward, but he ducks away)

VIRGINIE
You cannot claim that which is mine!

(She lunges again, but he hits her solidly in the face. She drops to all fours)

JEAN
STOP THIS!

(She tries to rise, snarling in pain. He kicks her in the stomach, rolling her over. He pounces on her, holding her down)

JEAN
I do not want to hurt you!

VIRGINIE
Let me go!

JEAN
No!

VIRGINIE
I'll slice your throat out!

JEAN
You're not winning my favor, cherie. Throw away the knife.

VIRGINIE
Burn in hell.

JEAN
Throw it away, and I'll let you go.

(Beat. She tosses the knife away)

JEAN
There.

(They both rise. She makes a move to go for the knife, but he grabs it first)

JEAN
Calmer now?

VIRGINIE
As a quiet river. Give me my knife and I'll show you.

JEAN
I've tasted as much of your wrath as I mean to today. *(He grabs a rag off the table, holding it to his bleeding face)* In time, you will understand why I did what I did.

VIRGINIE
Leave me.

JEAN
You don't want that.

VIRGINIE
What I did to your face should tell you exactly what I want.

JEAN
You do love me. I know you do.

VIRGINIE
Once. Never again.

JEAN
Then why do I still live?

VIRGINIE
Because you're faster than I am.

JEAN
Your spell, I mean. *(Beat. He holds up the hand he cut in Act I)* You said I'd be cursed if I betrayed you.

VIRGINIE
I never said what would happen. But now, you will find out.

JEAN
I don't fear your curses.

VIRGINIE
Because you are a braggart and a fool.

JEAN
I think a witch, a real witch, wouldn't need a knife to finish me.

VIRGINIE
Who said I wanted you dead?

(Beat)

JEAN
You've given me a few scars to add to my collection, nothing more.

VIRGINIE
Tell yourself that, Chastel. It will not make it true.

JEAN
Your rage will pass. You will see.

VIRGINIE
I'll see you beg forgiveness like a dog first.

JEAN
I do not beg.

VIRGINIE
You did the day we met, and you will again. *(She walks to the door, opens it)* I helped you…a stranger with a bloody arm and some coins. You stole a kiss from me that night.

JEAN
I remember.

VIRGINIE
I should've slapped you then, and never opened this door to you again. You awoke something inside me, something I'd not felt since I lost my Marcel. You had his wildness....the wildness of the natural world. Look at you now, a silken fop concerned about what men will think...men who you despise. I thought it was because you were like me, a creature of the woods. But no...you hated them because you wanted to be one of them, and they wouldn't let you. Petty, pathetic, and weak.

JEAN
You do not know me.

VIRGINIE
I have laid with you, run my fingers over your bare skin. I heard the secrets you breathe in your sleep. I held you and thought you were mine. You played me for a fool.

JEAN
Never.

VIRGINIE
Get out.

JEAN
What I did, I did to protect us both.

VIRGINIE
Go!

(He stabs her knife into the table, then goes to her)

JEAN
You still have your livres.

VIRGINIE
Yes.

JEAN
If you care so little for me and the ways of man, why
not give them to me?

(She glares at him)

JEAN
Spit on me all you like, but you're wants are no
different from mine.

VIRGINIE
I keep my pay if only to spite you.

JEAN
Tell yourself that. It will not make it true.

*(She spits at his feet. He walks to the doorway, about
to leave. He stares at her)*

JEAN
Au revoir.

*(For a moment, it looks as though they might kiss. She
places her hand on his chest, then pushes him out the
door. She slams it behind him. Lights fade)*

SCENE SEVEN

(Later. VIRGINIE is drinking wine. She wanders around her shack, touching each of the animals as she passes them. She finds herself in front of the bear. She touches his muzzle)

VIRGINIE
You...all teeth and claws and fur and not a brain in your skull...not a creature for thinking...you're savage and vicious. You ran when you needed to run, and you fought when you needed to fight. You pulled fish from rivers, clawed down beehives, and ate carrion when you had to. No pride there, no concerns. You did whatever you had to to survive, and never thought a thing beyond that. Just live and to hell with all the rest. To hell with the rest!! *(She drinks)* I should have been as wise as you... *(Beat)*...in love not just once in this life, but twice? ...unluckiest woman walking the earth...*(She pats the bear)* You knew my Marcel but briefly, and your meeting was not a friendly one, so you must trust

me when I tell you he was a good man...he wanted nothing more than me. He didn't care a whit for money or honor or...just me. Just me, just me, just me. *(She looks the bear in the eyes)* Never thought I'd love again, but...you catch the scent of some man...and you like it. You want to breathe it into your skin. You want to taste him on your lips when you wake. And it's good. You fight and you laugh and you make love like demons...and for just a moment, the space between one heartbeat and the next, nothing else exists. Just you and him and you are one. *(Beat)* Hard for any creature to survive alone in this world. *(Beat. She drinks again)* But there's nothing lasts forever in this world. Not the cities or the seas or the stones of the earth. And the fools...fools die quick...unless they learn...*(She touches the bear's face)* What say you, Gaspard? Do you think I've learned?

(Lights fade)

SCENE EIGHT

(Later. A few days, perhaps a few weeks. The cottage seems different. VIRGINIE has lit several candles about. She is wearing a hood. She opens the window, letting the breeze in. The beginning light of moon-rise slowly spills into the room. The of a strong wind outside. VIRGINIE sits in a chair, lowering her head. After a bit, her head snaps up. Then, JEAN staggers in. He no longer wears his fancy clothes, and seems ill)

JEAN
Help me...

VIRGINIE
I told you.

JEAN
The pain...you did this!

VIRGINIE
Yes.

JEAN
Stop it! Please!

VIRGINIE
I said I'd hear you beg again.

JEAN
Yes, goddammit! I'll say it on my knees if I must!

VIRGINIE
You must.

JEAN
(Staggering to his knees) Whatever this is, end it. I beg you.

VIRGINIE
Does it hurt?

JEAN
Yes!

VIRGINIE
Does it feel like your skin is on fire, like your every muscle is ripped and torn?

JEAN
Yes! YES!

VIRGINIE
You deserve worse. And you will get it.

(She grabs JEAN and pulls his head back. She then pours a vial down his throat. He coughs and gags)

JEAN
Christ...what was that...?

VIRGINIE
Henbane. Sevenbark. Other things. Older things.

JEAN
(Trying to stand, struggling not to retch) You... poisoned me...

VIRGINIE
Only if I got my mix wrong. And I never get it
wrong.

JEAN
Then what...?

(She grabs his face)

VIRGINIE
I wanted to, Chastel. Oh yes. As I ground the
weeds, I thought of you choking and dying.
Savored it, even. *(She pushes him over)* All day,
you've felt it, yes? The fever, the burning...here.
(She grabs his hand) Where I cut you. Where we
made our bond.

JEAN
You cursed me.

VIRGINIE
Aye. And earlier than you know. Now come.

*(She helps him rise, lays him on her table. He's too
weak to fight)*

VIRGINIE
There you are, lamb. Rest. You've a long night ahead
of you.

*(He manages to pull a pistol out of his coat. VIRGINIE
easily wrenches it away)*

VIRGINIE
A gift from my suitor?

(JEAN fights back a scream of pain)

VIRGINIE
Hush, pet. The pain will pass soon.

JEAN
...when I die?

VIRGINIE
I said I'd not poisoned you.

JEAN
Then what is this!?

VIRGINIE
The pain you feel...that is your own guilt made manifest, with a little help from the herbs I put in your cut hand weeks ago.

JEAN
You soul-less witch...

VIRGINIE
I know a thing about a thing. What I made you drink tonight...that will take the pain from you in a moment.

(JEAN suddenly lurches up, then vomits in a bucket)

VIRGINIE
Ah. There it is.

(JEAN is still weak, but regaining his strength)

JEAN
All Hells...that is what death tastes like.

VIRGINIE
You see? More sturdy on your feet. Still...

(She puts the pistol in her cloak)

VIRGINIE
...I'll be keeping this gift you brought me.

(He pulls a knife from his boot)

VIRGINIE
But you seem to have brought another.

JEAN
Tell me what you've done to me.

VIRGINIE
Mayhap.

JEAN
TELL ME!

VIRGINIE
Would you believe it, I wonder. Or would it be
better to just let you find out yourself?

JEAN
(As he speaks, he recovers more) I awoke and found
myself weak. I ate, I checked my pheasant traps, but
as the day wore on, I grew sicker and sicker. Soon I
was back in bed and then...the dreams.

VIRGINIE
(Smiling) Oui.

JEAN
...the things I saw...the things I saw myself doing...
a world in crimson... *(He stops, realizing the pain has
passed)* You summoned me here.

VIRGINIE
I did.

JEAN
Why?

VIRGINIE
Not an easy question to answer.

JEAN
Vengeance? Is that it? Revenge against the man who

made you wealthy?

VIRGINIE
Gods, are you truly such a dullard? I care nothing for the King's gold!

JEAN
Then why help me?

VIRGINIE
Why do you think?! *(Beat)* It is a curse to fall in love.

JEAN
So then...?

VIRGINIE
I wanted a mate. I wanted you.

JEAN
All your talk of belonging to no man...

VIRGINIE
Love isn't ownership, you fool. It's...simpler than that. More primal, more rare.

JEAN
Then why curse me, cherie? *(He goes to her)* I do love you. You know I do.

VIRGINIE
Mayhap. But you love yourself more.

JEAN
Because I said I was the one who made the Beast? That was to protect you just as it was to protect me!

VIRGINIE
Do I strike you as a woman who needs protection, Chastel?!

JEAN
I DON'T KNOW! Christ above, you're all but a
madwoman! One moment you're threatening death,
the next…How am I supposed to know what you
are but in the moment?!

VIRGINIE
The moment is all we have! It is all anyone has!

JEAN
(Grabbing her by the shoulder) Then who are you,
right now?! In this very moment, who are you!?

VIRGINIE
I…

JEAN
TELL ME!

*(She grabs him by the throat. He is shocked by her
strength. She throws him away from her)*

VIRGINIE
This moment depends entirely on you.

*(She takes his pistol and sets it on the table. Taking a
sack from a drawer, she sets it next to the pistol)*

VIRGINIE
You know what this is?

JEAN
The coin I gave you, from the King.

VIRGINIE
Oui. Every livre remains. I've not spent even an
ounce of it.

JEAN
Why?

VIRGINIE
At first, I did not know. I would stare at it, wondering what I might buy with it. But something held me back. Now I know why...for this moment. For you.

JEAN
I do not understand.

VIRGINIE
No, I imagine you don't. *(Beat)* It is quite simple, mon chere. I want you to prove me wrong. You say you love me, you say that what you do is for my benefit...and I want to believe you, but I don't. Oh, you may mean the words as you say them, but words are what we say, not what we do. *(She takes the sack, shakes it)* How much of your reward have you spent already, hmmm? How many fancy suits, fancy meals, and other luxuries? And with every bauble, you became one of...them. One of the soft, weak sheep that live in cities and wring their hands over who said what about who. I didn't spend mine because what need have I for such things? But you...? You've a taste for fine things now, and there's nothing worse than that.

JEAN
You're...giving me this?

VIRGINIE
Giving? No. Do beasts give to each other? If you want this, you much take it from me. *(She nudges the gun towards him)*

JEAN
I'll not kill you, Virginie.

VIRGINIE
Will you not? Do you love me more than your creature comforts? More than everything 150 livres can
buy you?

JEAN
Yes.

VIRGINIE
I don't believe you. I believe you did this, did
all this, for naught but Jean Chastel. Those who
hated you now worship you. You've been honored
by the King himself! And I? I am the only one
alive who knows the truth of it. Why not kill me,
take the coins, and live the rest of your days a
wealthy man?

JEAN
That is not what I want.

VIRGINIE
Liar! Every damned word that slips from your mouth
is worth nothing!

JEAN
Virginie...

VIRGINIE
A man doesn't betray the woman he loves! A man
stays true, holds to his words and his vows, because
it would never occur to him to do aught else! But
you are no man, hero of Gévaudan. You are a selfish,
lying son of a whore.

(He closes on her, his anger rising)

JEAN
Careful, woman.

VIRGINIE
Go on then. Threaten me. I can see the tail tucked between your legs.

JEAN
Virginie...

VIRGINIE
I'll speak, Chastel. I'll tell the tale to every soul in the province.

JEAN
Enough! *(He grabs the pistol, pointing it at her)*

VIRGINIE
There it is. Pull the trigger, silence me, and take your coin.

JEAN
I said enough!

VIRGINIE
Just take my corpse and bury it out there. Who would mourn the witch of the woods? Certainly not you.

(He stares at her for a bit, then kisses her. They embrace)

VIRGINIE
Jean, I...

(He grabs the pistol and shoots her in the chest. She drops behind the table)

JEAN
Je suis désolé, ma cherie.

(He sets the gun down, truly saddened)

JEAN
Virginie...I did love you. Truly. But how could I

trust you? How could I ever trust you?

(Beat. He takes the sack of coins)

JEAN
I hope you are free now...free of whatever lunacy cursed you in this life. Au revoir.

(He goes to the door. The sound of a wolf growling is heard. JEAN stops. He looks around, but it is unclear where the sound is coming from. VIRGINIE rises from behind the table, a bloody spot on her shirt. Her appearance may have altered slightly...yellow eyes, subtle claws, etc)

VIRGINIE
You never listen, Jean. You never listen.

JEAN
Qu'est-ce que tu fais...?

VIRGINIE
I said before...only a silver bullet.

(He reaches for the door. VIRGINIE runs to him and throws him away from it)

VIRGINIE
No, no, no, mon chere. I'm not done with you yet.

(He brandishes his knife)

VIRGINIE
That will do you no more good than the pistol.

JEAN
What...what are you?!

VIRGINIE
Can you not tell? I am the Beast of Gévaudan.

JEAN
There is no…it's a story, nothing more!

VIRGINIE
So sure, are you?

JEAN
C'est impossible!

VIRGINIE
I knew it. I knew you'd choice the coin over me.

JEAN
Just let me go.

VIRGINIE
I watched you for months, Chastel. Months. Stalking you as you hunted, watched you from the woods… You were an outcast, just like me. You loved these woods as I love them. You were everything I wanted.

JEAN
What do you…?

VIRGINIE
It was not a choice I made lightly, but I am not a lone wolf. Never was. I don't like hunting alone. And so…

JEAN
That thing I shot in the woods…that thing that bit me…

VIRGINIE
Just a taste, love. A little nip. I knew you'd likely run to the only place that might take you in and help you. *(She gestures to the room)*

JEAN
You set a trap for me.

VIRGINIE
I did. You are not the only hunter here.

JEAN
Christ, why not just tell me!?

VIRGINIE
I had to know if you were truly worthy of the gift I gave you! A month to know you, to learn what sort of heart beats in your chest…all for nothing.

JEAN
The bite…does that mean I am like you?

VIRGINIE
You would have been, had you lived long enough.

(Beat. JEAN holds up the knife again)

JEAN
Stay back.

VIRGINIE
Tomorrow, the next full moon will rise. It would have been the first time you turned. You would have loved it, the world of scents and tastes and beautiful nights that never end. Forever fierce and forever free.

JEAN
I said stay back!

VIRGINIE
You truly do not know how much I wanted this… wanted you. But in the end, you have a man's heart, Jean Chastel. A man's weakness.

JEAN
I have hunted every beast of France and survived. I will survive you.

VIRGINIE
Think you so?

(He charges her. She dodges his knife easily, throwing him against a while)

VIRGINIE
Three years ago, the bastards of Gévaudan killed my Marcel. I never knew who, or even how they did it. He'd been a wolf when they did, and they took his head before I found him. I went mad then, and swore to kill any and all who came too close to my woods. Over a hundred fell to my claws these last years.

JEAN
You were...too wild...too savage.

VIRGINIE
I never intended to bring the King's wrath down upon me, but c'est la vie.

JEAN
I will help you.

(Beat)

VIRGINIE
What?

JEAN
You've but to let me live, and I can help you as Marcel helped you. I know these woods as well as he did, mayhap better.

VIRGINIE
Do not speak of him to me!

JEAN
We can hunt together, as wolves do. Smart, cunning. The King believes the Beast is dead...so

let him! *(He moves very slowly towards her)* Virginie! You went mad in your grief, ma cherie. Love me as you loved him, and your madness will pass. We will be a lone wolves no more.

(Beat. They stare at each other for a bit. Suddenly, VIRGINIE begins to laugh)

VIRGINIE
God's blood, Chastel! The balls on you! It is a wonder you can stand straight!

(He smiles)

JEAN
You know I am right.

VIRGINIE
I know you are a liar.

JEAN
Look in my eyes and tell me if I'm lying now.

(He grabs her, bringing her face to his. She stares into his eyes. She touches his face)

JEAN
I am as much a wolf as you.

(She kisses him. They hold each other in a passionate embrace. He begins to kiss her neck)

VIRGINIE
Jean...my Jean...

(As her ardor grows, she suddenly and savagely rips her claws across JEAN's throat. He stares at her, shocked and bleeding out)

VIRGINIE
I'm sorry, love. But a man who betrays once will

betray again.

(As he struggles for life, she lifts him onto her table)

VIRGINIE
There you are. There you are. It is almost over.
There...

*(She strokes his hair as he dies. When he is gone, she
holds his hand and weeps for a bit)*

VIRGINIE
I'll take you to your home, mon chere. Set a fire
and burn you inside it. None will ever know what
happened here. None will know. (She kisses his
palm, smelling his hand) I will miss your scent.

*(She sets his hand down and begins to collect some
items for burning. Outside, a single wolf howls. Soon,
it is joined by a chorus of wolves. She joins in softly,
in her sorrow, as the lights fade)*

END OF PLAY

ABOUT THE PLAYWRIGHT

Joseph Zettelmaier is a Michigan-based playwright and four-time nominee for the Steinberg/American Theatre Critics Association Award for best new play, first in 2006 for ALL CHILDISH THINGS, then in 2007 for LANGUAGE LESSONS, in 2010 for IT CAME FROM MARS and in 2012 for ALL CHILDISH THINGS. Other plays include SALVAGE, THE GRAVEDIGGER—A FRANKENSTEIN PLAY, NORTHERN AGGRESSION, DR. SEWARD'S DRACULA, INVASIVE SPECIES, THE SCULLERY MAID, NIGHT BLOOMING, and EBENEZER.

POINT OF ORIGIN won Best Locally Created Script 2002 from the Ann Arbor News, and THE STILLNESS BETWEEN BREATHS also won Best New Play 2005 from the Oakland Press. THE STILLNESS BETWEEN BREATHS and IT CAME FROM MARS were selected to appear in the National New Play Network's Festival of New Plays. He also co-authored Flyover, USA: Voices From Men of the Midwest at the Williamston Theatre (Winner of the 2009 Thespie Award for Best New Script). He also adapted CHRISTMAS CAROL'D for the Performance Network.

IT CAME FROM MARS was a recipient of 2009's Edgerton Foundation New American Play Award, and won Best New Script 2010 from the Lansing State Journal. His play ALL CHILDISH THINGS won the Edgerton Foundation New American Play Award in 2011.

Joseph is a founding member of the Roustabout Theatre Company and an Associate Artist at First Folio Shakespeare, an Artistic Ambassador to the National New Play Network, and an adjunct lecturer at Eastern Michigan University, where he teaches Dramatic Composition.

AVAILABLE PLAYS BY
JOSEPH ZETTELMAIER

IT CAME FROM MARS

THE DECADE DANCE

DR. SEWARD'S DRACULA

THE GRAVEDIGGER
A FRANKENSTEIN PLAY

CAMPFIRE

DEAD MAN'S SHOES

THE SCULLERY MAID

ALL CHILDISH THINGS

NORTHERN AGGRESSION
(AND THE CREEK DON'T RISE)

EBENEZER
A CHRISTMAS PLAY

STAGE FRIGHT
A HORROR ANTHOLOGY

For information about production rights, visit:
www.jzettelmaier.com

MORE PLAYS FROM SORDELET INK

A TALE OF TWO CITIES
by Christoper M Walsh
adapted from the novel by Charles Dickens

THE COUNT OF MONTE CRISTO
by Christoper M Walsh
adapted from the novel by Alexandre Dumas

THE MOONSTONE
by Robert Kauzlaric
adapted from the novel by Wilkie Collins

HER MAJESTY'S WILL
by Robert Kauzlaric
adapted from the novel by David Blixt

SEASON ON THE LINE
by Shawn Pfautsch
adapted from Herman Melville's MOBY-DICK

ACTION MOVIE: THE PLAY
by Joe Foust and Richard Ragsdale

ONCE A PONZI TIME
by Joe Foust

EVE OF IDES
by David Blixt

Visit www.sordeletink.com for more!

THE MYSTERY OF CENTRAL PARK

A rejected marriage proposal and the corpse of a dead beauty confound Dick Treadwell's hopes for happiness, until his beloved Penelope sets him a task: she will marry him if he solves— *the Mystery of Central Park!*

EVA, THE ADVENTURESS

Nellie Bly's ripped-from-the-headlines novel of a poor girl determined to revenge herself upon the world, only to find that, in the battle between love and revenge, only one can triumph.

NEW YORK BY NIGHT

Setting out to solve the bold diamond robbery, millionaire detective Lionel Dangerfield finds himself in competition with Ruby Sharpe, daring young reporter for the *New York Planet*. Will "The Danger" solve the case before Ruby can steal the story—and his heart?

ALTA LYNN, M.D.

A prank goes awry and Alta Lynn finds herself wed against her will. Leaving love behind, she throws herself into the study of medicine, only to find that love has other plans for her!

WAYNE'S FAITHFUL SWEETHEART

Beautiful Dorette Lover is rescued from poverty when she finds work as an artist's model. That same day she witnesses a seeming murder. To protect the man accused, she agrees to become his bride — only to fall desperately in love with him!

LITTLE LUCKIE

Luckie Thurlow longs for to be accepted by society and gain the man she loves. But she harbors a dark secret — she is the daughter of the murderous Gypsy Queen, who plans to use Luckie to gain her own revenge!

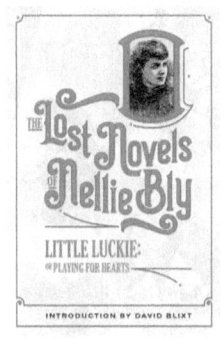

IN LOVE WITH A STRANGER

Kit Clarendon is in love! Trouble is, she doesn't know her love's name. But she is determined to track him down and force him to love her! A wild pursuit filled with disguises, desperate deeds, and declarations of love as Kit determines to go through fire and water to win him!

THE LOVE OF THREE GIRLS

An heiress in disguise, a factory girl with dreams of wealth, and a sweet child of charity are forced into rivalry when they all fall in love with the same man! Murder, fever, fallen women, and a desperate villain conspire against — *the love of three girls!*

INTO THE MADHOUSE

Never before collected! "Who is this insane girl?" asked other papers, completely taken in by Nellie Bly's plan to infiltrate Blackwell's Island. The complete reporting surrounding her daring expose, including details not included in her initial accounts and her scathing rebuttal of the doctors' excuses!

NELLIE BLY'S WORLD - Vol. 1
1887-1888

Bly's complete reporting, collected for the very first time! Starting with the stunt that made hers a household name, Nellie Bly spends her first year at the New York World going undercover to expose frauds, sharpsters and boodlers, interviewing Belva Lockwood and Hangman Joe, and tackling Phelps the Lobbyist!

NELLIE BLY'S WORLD - Vol. 2
1889-1890

Bly's complete reporting, collected for the very first time! Nellie buys a baby, has herself followed by a detective and arrested, interviews Helen Keller, champion boxer John Sullivan, and convicted would-be killer Eva Hamilton, all before setting out on her greatest stunt of all, a race around the world!

COMING SOON:

NELLIE BLY'S WORLD, Vol. 3 & 4
NELLIE BLY'S DISPATCHES, Vol. 1 & 2
NELLIE BLY's JOURNALS, Vol. 1 & 2

ALL FROM SORDELET INK

Books by David Blixt

Nellie Bly
What Girls Are Good For
Charity Girl
Clever Girl

The Star-Cross'd Series
The Master Of Verona
Voice Of The Falconer
Fortune's Fool
The Prince's Doom
Varnish'd Faces: Star-Cross'd Short Stories

Will & Kit
Her Majesty's Will

The Colossus Series
Colossus: Stone & Steel
Colossus: The Four Emperors

Eve of Ides - a play

NON-FICTION
Shakespeare's Secrets: Romeo & Juliet
Tomorrow, and Tomorrow: Essays on Macbeth
Fighting Words

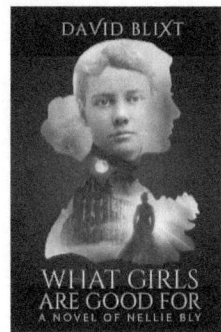

WHAT GIRLS ARE GOOD FOR
A NOVEL OF NELLIE BLY

Nellie Bly has the story of a lifetime. But will she survive to tell it?

Based on the real-life events of the tiny Pennsylvania spitfire who refused to let the world change her, and changed the world instead.

CHARITY GIRL
A NELLIE BLY NOVELETTE

Fresh from her escape from Blackwell's Island, Nellie Bly investigates the doctors who buy and sell babies in Victorian New York. Based on real events and her own reporting, Nellie Bly asks the devastating question—what becomes of babies?

CLEVER GIRL
A NELLIE BLY NOVELLA

A blizzard has frozen all of New York, and Nellie Bly is going stir-crazy when she and Colonel Cockerill plot out her most daring undercover assignment yet: she's going to trap the most crooked man in politics, Edward R. Phelps, the self-styled "King" of the Albany lobby.

COMING SOON:

STUNT GIRL

A NOVEL OF NELLIE BLY

BY DAVID BLIXT

www.ingramcontent.com/pod-product-compliance
Lightning Source LLC
Chambersburg PA
CBHW020249150626
46552CB00020B/730